Salem noticed Sabrina's history book on the floor.

"Sabrina!" Salem shouted. "Wait! You forgot something!" He jumped off the bed, not looking where he was going. With a *plop!* Salem fell right into Sabrina's history book! He felt as if he were falling very, very slowly. Then he realized he was shrinking.

Salem twisted and turned. "A cat always lands on his feet," he told himself. "The trouble is, I don't know *where* I'm going to land! I don't even know where the ground is!"

Whoosh! Salem plunged into a deep bank of snow. *Brr!* It was cold! Then someone grabbed him by the back of his neck. "Poor cat," said a kind voice. "You'd better be careful where you step. Here you are, safe and sound."

Salem felt the man set him down on solid ground. He blinked snow out of his eyes and looked up in suprise. He knew this tall man. He was George Washington!

Where am I? Salem wondered. *When am I?*

Sabrina, The Teenage Witch™
Salem's Tails™

#1 Cat TV
#2 Teacher's Pet
#3 You're History!
Salem Goes to Rome (tie-in)

Available from MINSTREL Books

YOU'RE HISTORY

Brad & Barbara Strickland

Based on Characters Appearing in Archie Comics

And based upon the television series
Sabrina, The Teenage Witch
Created for television by Nell Scovell
Developed for television by Jonathan Schmock

Illustrated by Mark Dubowski

Published by POCKET BOOKS
New York London Toronto Sydney Tokyo Singapore

A MINSTREL PAPERBACK *Original*

A Minstrel Book published by
POCKET BOOKS, a division of Simon & Schuster Inc.
1230 Avenue of the Americas, New York, NY 10020

Sabrina, The Teenage Witch: Salem's Tails
Based on Characters Appearing in Archie Comics
And the Television Series Created by Nell Scovell
Developed for Television by Jonathan Schmock

Salem quotes taken from the following episodes:
"Halloween Story" written by Nell Scovell
"Sabrina Gets Her License—Part 1"
written by Miriam Trogdan

ISBN: 0-671-02104-4

First Minstrel Books printing December 1998

10 9 8 7 6 5 4 3 2 1

Cover photo by Pat Hill Studio

Printed in the U.S.A.

To all our friends at Egleston Children's Hospital
—happy reading!

"Double, double toil and trouble."

—*Macbeth*, by William Shakespeare

"Bill Shakespeare stole that from us. What a hack."

—*Salem*

Chapter 1

Sabrina Spellman looked up from her book. "Salem," she said, "would you help me study for my history test?"

Salem was the Spellmans' black cat. He lived with Sabrina and her two aunts, who were not ordinary aunts. They were witches. That was all right, because Salem was not an ordinary pet. For one thing, he could talk. Salem lay on Sabrina's bed with his eyes half closed, thinking about what Sabrina had said. "Why should I help you?" he asked.

"Because I need help," Sabrina told him. "We have a test on five chapters of American history tomorrow. It's hard for me to remember all these names and dates."

Salem sniffed. Before he became a cat, he had been a powerful warlock—a male witch. He had one suggestion. "Just use magic to give you the answers in class," he said. "After all, you *are* a teenage witch."

Sabrina shook her head. "I can't just use magic to give me answers. That would be cheating," she told him. "I have to be able to think up the answers on my own. Come on. At least you can quiz me. Ask me some questions about history."

"Sorry," Salem said. He was feeling lazy and sleepy. "I'm not in the mood."

"Wait until you want a favor from me," Sabrina warned him. Then she said in a sly voice, "I know why you won't help. You can't. You don't know much history."

Salem grinned at her. It was a cat grin, but it was a grin. "Nice try, but it won't work. You aren't going to trick me that way. As a matter of fact, I know *lots* of history. I know *all* the names and places and dates. That's because I lived through history!"

Sabrina looked thoughtful. "Hmm. Now, that's an idea."

"What is?" asked Salem.

"You said you lived through history," Sabrina said. "Well, that's just what I need—a way to make history come alive." She looked down at her American history book. It was very thick, and almost every page had pictures on it. "If I could make this book come alive, it could quiz me on the history that's in it. That wouldn't be cheating, but it would help me study."

Salem yawned. He did not think much of that idea. "I wouldn't try that if I were you," he told Sabrina. "First, you don't know what a living book might do. It might run through the house dropping periods and question marks all over the place. It might flap its covers and fly away like a bird. It might—"

"I get the picture," Sabrina said.

"Second," said Salem, "it isn't the *book* that should seem alive to you. It's *history.*"

"You're right," Sabrina said slowly, looking as if she were thinking it over.

Salem's cat-grin grew wider. "Of course I am. I am older than you, I am better educated than you, and most of all, I am a cat. Cats are perfect."

"Then why do you always complain about being one?" Sabrina asked.

Salem frowned. "Because it wasn't my

idea," he said. "The Council of Witches turned me into a cat for no reason at all."

"They had a reason," Sabrina pointed out. "You tried to take over the world."

"Well, they turned me into a cat for *practically* no reason at all," Salem replied. "And while a cat is a very noble animal, being one has drawbacks. How would *you* like to have a litterbox? It's embarrassing!"

"I wouldn't like that," Sabrina admitted. "And I don't think I could ever learn to eat raw fish."

"Ahhh, fish . . ." Salem trailed off dreamily, then shook his head. "This isn't getting your studying done."

With a sigh, Sabrina said, "I know." She thought for a few seconds. Then she smiled. "And now I know how magic can help me. I won't make the book come to life, and I won't cheat. Instead, I'll become part of the book!"

"Oh," Salem said. "You're going to turn yourself into a comma. What a great plan. I think you've gone a little cuckoo."

"No, silly," Sabrina told him. "I'm going to cast a spell on my history book. Then I'm going to jump right into it. I'll meet all the people we're studying about and make sure I know all about them. That way I'll be sure to pass the test!"

Salem sat up. His tail lashed in alarm. "Sabrina, you know witches are not supposed to change history!"

"Don't worry," she said. "I'm not casting a spell on *history*—just on my book. I'm not going to change anything in the real world."

"Oh," Salem said. He lay down again and started to wash his paws. "That might be all right."

Sabrina got up from her desk. She opened her history book and put it on the floor. Then, standing over it, she thought up a spell.

"Let me in to take a look
at the history within this book.
Make it all seem real to me
so I'll remember history!"

Then Sabrina pointed at the book. Something started to happen. The book began to shiver. The pages fluttered. A blue glow surrounded them. "How's that?" Sabrina asked.

Salem paused in his washing. "Not bad," he said. "I could have done better, of course—"

"Well, if it helps me on the test, it's good enough," Sabrina told him. "Here goes!" She bent her knees. She took a deep breath. Then she jumped, as if she were going to land right on the book.

Except as she jumped, she began to shrink. Sabrina became smaller and smaller, until she was no larger than one of the pictures in her book. Salem watched as she jumped right into the story of America.

Sabrina landed feet-first and disappeared into the pages, just like someone jumping from a diving board into a pool. The words on the page rippled back and forth before they grew still again.

"Well," Salem said. "I hope she has a good time!"

He settled down, wrapped his tail around himself for comfort, and soon fell asleep. He dreamed of chasing mice. He dreamed of drinking cream, but he did not start to purr until he dreamed about taking over the world.

Then he purred like crazy.

He had been sleeping for an hour or

two when a noise woke him. "What's that?" he yelped in surprise, sitting up. Then he saw the book on the floor. It was flapping, flipping, and fluttering. It was hopping up and down.

"Yipes!" Salem said. "I hope Sabrina's not in trouble!"

Blue light flashed out of the pages. Then a tiny figure rose from the book. It grew larger and larger as it flew through the air. Salem watched as Sabrina grew back to her normal size. She landed on the floor with a light thump. "Whee!" she said. "That was fun!"

"Welcome home," Salem said crossly. "You woke me up."

"Don't be a grump," Sabrina told him. "I wouldn't have jumped into the book if you had helped me!"

"I hope you got all your studying done," Salem said.

Sabrina scratched his ears. "I sure did. I think I'm ready for the test." She looked at the clock. "Wow, it's late! I'd better go right to bed so I'll be rested tomorrow."

"Oh, wonderful," Salem said. "You wake *me* up and then *you* get to go to sleep."

"Sorry," Sabrina told him. "But you'd still be snoozing if you hadn't decided to nap in my room."

"Throw me out!" Salem said, making his voice sad. "Cast me into the storm! Take me away from the only home I have!" He began to sob.

"What's wrong?" Sabrina asked.

"I'm breaking my heart!" Salem wailed. "Hold a tissue for me, please. I want to blow my nose."

Sabrina said, "You can stay inside, you silly cat. In fact, you can go right back to sleep. That's what I'm going to do!"

That seemed like a good idea to Salem. A few minutes later both of them were sound asleep.

Salem did not wake up until he heard Sabrina shriek.

"What is it? What's wrong?" he asked, leaping up in fright. "Is the house on fire? Did your aunts learn you've been borrowing their sweaters? What?"

"It's morning, and I'm late!" Sabrina yelled. "I forgot to set my clock!" She dashed out. Salem heard the shower running. After a few seconds, Sabrina ran back in. She recited a magic spell, pointed at herself, and with a flash she was dressed and ready for school.

"You'd better have breakfast!" Salem warned.

"I'll get some toast and peanut butter to eat on the way!" Sabrina said. "Gotta go!" She rushed out the door.

Just then Salem noticed her history book. It was still on the floor. "Sabrina!" he shouted. "Wait! You forgot something!" He jumped off the bed.

He did not look where he was jumping. Everything suddenly felt strange. Salem felt as if he were falling very, very slowly. Then he realized he was shrinking. He looked down—oh, no!

With a *plop!* Salem fell right into Sabrina's history book! Everything went dark.

Chapter 2

Salem fell through the dark. Wind whistled past his whiskers. He twisted and turned. "A cat always lands on his feet," he told himself. "The trouble is, I don't know *where* I'm going to land! I don't even know where the ground is!"

The ground rushed up to meet him. It was flat and seemed to be white. "It looks like snow," Salem said. "I hope it's deep. I *really* hope it's soft!"

Whoosh! He plunged into a deep bank of snow. *Brr!* It was cold! Snow cut off the air. It was hard to breathe. A shaken Salem quickly began to dig his way up. He made a cat tunnel in the snow bank. He gasped for air, but snow filled his nose and his mouth. He was scared.

Then someone grabbed him by the back of his neck. He felt himself being pulled out of the snow bank. The icy clumps of snow fell away from him as he rose. He came out coughing, and he gulped a deep breath of air. "Poor cat," said a kind voice. "You'd better be careful where you step. Here you are, safe and sound."

Salem felt the man set him down on solid ground. He blinked snow out of his eyes and looked up. It was dark, but cats can see in the dark. He blinked his eyes again, this time in surprise. He knew this tall man. He was George Washington!

Where am I? Salem wondered. *When am I?* Then he saw that George Washington was wearing a uniform. Salem knew then that he was in the part of the history book that told about the American Revolution. He wondered how he would get out.

Salem looked around. It was a dark winter evening. He sat on a path that had been shoveled clear of snow, but on both sides the snow was piled high. That was where he had fallen. It was a good thing that General Washington had picked him up. Salem stood up and twitched some snow out of his fur.

General Washington walked slowly away from Salem. He headed for a little wooden house. Salem was shivering from the cold and the snow. He decided

he had better get inside to warm up, so he dashed after the general. Washington opened the door and stepped inside the hut. Salem slipped inside just behind him, and the general closed the door.

A small red fire burned in a fireplace, and a couple of candles gave a dim light, but the inside of the hut was still very cold. General Washington slumped into a wooden chair. He looked tired and upset. He closed his eyes for a second. When he opened them and saw Salem sitting with his back to the fire, he smiled. "Well, cat," he said, "this is not a very happy Christmas, is it?"

Christmas, thought Salem. *It's Christmas, and it's some time during the American Revolution.*

Then he remembered why Sabrina had cast a spell on the history book. *I think*

I see how to get back home, Salem thought. *I have to know all the facts about history and be sure they are right. If I can figure history out, then I can get through the book and get home again! Well, a simple quiz should be easy for me. I know history because I lived through it!*

General Washington put a hand over his eyes. "Cat, I am tired," he said. "And so are my men. I hope my poor army can hold together through this long winter."

Salem felt uneasy. What if he *couldn't* figure everything out? Would he be trapped in the book forever? He shivered.

"If only we could cross the river," General Washington said. "One victory at Trenton could make a big difference."

"Trenton?" Salem asked eagerly. "Trenton, New Jersey?"

General Washington looked up. He blinked in surprise. "A talking cat? I must be dreaming!"

Salem never let anyone except the Spellmans know he could talk. Now he thought fast. He said, "Yes, General, you are dreaming. Of course you are. After all, we both know that cats can't talk. Ha-ha-ha!"

With a little smile, General Washington said, "If I am dreaming, I need the sleep. I have been so worried these last few weeks I haven't rested very much. The weather is cruel and cold, and my soldiers are tired and hungry."

"But they would be warm and well-fed in Trenton," Salem said. He was starting to understand. This was a part of the history quiz. If he could remember history, he could tell General Washington what would be the best thing to do. The best thing would have to be what had really happened. Now, what did he remember about the Battle of Trenton?

"Let me see," Salem said. "Today is December 25, 1776. This is the American army camp close to—don't tell me. I can remember this." Salem frowned as he thought. "I've got it! Close to McKonkey's Ferry. Just across the Delaware River is the Hessian camp at Trenton. Am I right?"

"You're right, little dream cat," Washington said. "I think this would be a good time to strike. The Hessians have been celebrating Christmas with lots of food and music and dancing. They won't expect a battle. They will be tired from their celebration. I just don't know if my army can cross the river tonight and still fight tomorrow."

"Ah-hah!" Salem said. "General, your army *has* to cross the river and fight. They are starving and freezing, but the Hessians will have food, warm blankets, and good weapons. Your army could use all that. What you have to do is capture Trenton."

"The river is full of ice," General Washington said. "It will be hard to cross."

"Staying on this side of the river would be worse," Salem said, hopping up on George's lap. "I don't know what you will do, but I know what a cat would do."

"What is that, dream cat?" asked General Washington.

"A cat would pounce!" Salem answered. "When you have the mice all in a corner, you get ready, and then you pounce. You do it fast. You do it before the mice can think. That way you catch them all."

General Washington nodded. "Yes," he said, absently stroking the black cat. "If we attacked at dawn, we would catch all our Hessian mice in one place. They would be surprised. We would have to march straight into the town. The Hessians will have guards out, though."

"Yes, they will," Salem agreed. "Still, the guards have been celebrating. They will be sleepy. With surprise on your side, you can rush right into the town. You might be able to capture all the Hessian soldiers. That would be a great victory for the American army. You'd be on your way to winning the war. You could even take over the world! Oops!"

General Washington laughed. "I don't want to take over the world, cat. I only want to win our country's freedom."

"Then wake up," Salem said. "Close

your eyes and open them again, and then go and take your army across the river! You can do it!"

Washington closed his eyes. He opened them. He said to Salem, "Am I awake now?"

Salem only said, "Meow."

The general jumped out of his chair. He rushed to the door. Salem heard him giving quick orders: "Parade the troops! Get the boats ready! We are going to cross the Delaware and attack Trenton!" The general looked back. "Come with us, little cat. I have a feeling you may bring us good luck."

General Washington hurried down to the ferry. Salem followed him. He saw hundreds of American soldiers, dressed in tattered coats. They lined up. Salem saw some of them hauling cannons down to the river. Boats waited there. The river was gray and dark. Big pieces of ice floated in it. Salem could hear them bumping into the wooden boats—*Boom! Boom!*

Washington got into a boat, and Salem leaped in after him. "Push off!" the general said. His men used their oars, and the boat began to move. Some of the men had long poles. When chunks of ice blocked the way, these men pushed them aside. Slowly the boats crossed.

One of the men said, "It's late, General. We won't be across by midnight. It may be day before we can get to Trenton. The enemy will see us coming. Should we turn back?"

"No!" said General Washington. "We'll be like cats, and the Hessians will be the mice we chase. A cat wouldn't run away from mice, would he?"

"No, sir!" the man said, sounding happy.

"Then we will push on," Washington said. He reached down and scratched Salem's ears. "If we have good luck, we will take Trenton tomorrow. Tomorrow night our army will be safe, well-fed, and warm."

Crossing the river took hours. At last the boats crunched onto the shore. Washington stood. "Now let us gather our soldiers and our weapons," he said. "And may we win a great victory in Trenton today."

You will! Salem thought. He knew that the American army would take Trenton. They would also capture almost a thousand Hessian soldiers. The battle would be one of the turning points of the American Revolution. Soldiers would take heart from it. The Americans would have a great victory to celebrate. Salem knew that, in time, General Washington would get what he wanted. He would win his nation's freedom.

A happy Salem jumped off the boat and—

Oh, no! The ground disappeared! Once again, Salem was falling fast into the dark. . . .

Chapter 3

"This is like riding a roller coaster," Salem said as he fell. "The only thing wrong with that is I *hate* roller coasters! Why can't I fall into a nice, warm, sunny day?"

He was falling into a dark, cold night again. This time he felt himself crash into the branches of a tree. He shot out his claws and grabbed. "Ouch! Oof! Umph!" Finally his claws snagged a branch. For a second it bobbed up and down. "This could make me seasick," Salem wailed. "It could make me tree-sick!"

Then the limb came to rest. From the middle of the tree, Salem looked around. It was a dark, dark night. No snow lay on the ground below, but the trees had no leaves.

"Hmm," Salem said. "Feels like winter. It's cold, but not as cold as in General Washington's camp. I wonder if I'm farther south this time? What chapter of Sabrina's book have I landed in now?"

There was only one way to find out. Salem began to climb down the tree. It was tall, but he did not mind. "I've never found a tree yet that I couldn't get out of," he told himself. "Even if it takes me all night!"

It did not take him that long. He finally jumped from the tree trunk onto stiff, dry grass. A road wound past, and he walked

out onto it. He sat on the edge of the road. "What have we here?" he muttered. "A dirt road. That doesn't help much. I could be just about anywhere and any time. I'd better explore." He looked up at the sky.

He saw the stars of the Big Dipper hanging there. He followed the handle of the Big Dipper with his eyes until he spotted the North Star. "I might as well go north," Salem told himself. "I have four choices of direction. Since I'm lost, north is as good as any."

For a little while he walked. He heard sounds around him—the rustle of trees in the wind, the hoots of owls, the footsteps of small animals scurrying through the grass. At last he heard another sound. It was the sound of voices, several of them.

Salem crept ahead quietly. Ahead he could see a group of ten people standing in some tall brush near the road. He could hear one of the women saying, "I must go back! He's my son!"

A second woman said, "I know how you feel, but we can't go back. The patrol is out. If we're caught, you know what your master will do to you."

Master! thought Salem. *This must be a time before the Civil War. These people are slaves who are running away to the North. They want freedom!*

"I'll go back," the first woman whispered sadly.

A man added, "I'll go too. We are a family. I won't leave my son and wife behind in slavery."

The other woman had a strong voice. "You *can't* go back," she said. "If they catch you, they'll catch all of us. I'm sorry." She paused. "When did you last see little William?"

"About a mile back, when we rested last," the man said. He sounded as if he were about to cry. "He must have wandered off."

"I'll go look back aways," the woman said. "I'll find him."

"Oh, no," William's mother said. "You're our leader. You're our Moses. We can't follow the Railroad without you."

Salem had heard enough. He remembered that in the 1850s, slaves escaped to the North or to Canada by following the Underground Railroad. It was not a real railroad, and it was not underground. The Underground Railroad was made of different paths slaves could take to freedom. Along the way were "stations." These were houses owned by friendly people who wanted to help. They hid the slaves and gave them food as the runaways made their way North.

Salem turned and ran back the way he had come. He knew that the escaping slaves were heading north, so the lost boy, William, had to be in the other direction. Salem ran south as fast as he could.

When he had gone about a mile, he slowed. He listened with his cat ears. He heard a soft sound. It was a little boy crying. Salem followed the sound. When he could just see a small shape hiding beneath a bush, Salem said, "William?"

The little boy looked around. "Who's that?"

"I'm a friend," Salem said, keeping to the other side of the bush so the child couldn't see him.

William sniffled. "I went to sleep," he said. "We stopped to rest and I heard water. I wanted a drink. I fell asleep. Then they were all gone."

"They couldn't find you," Salem said. "They didn't leave you."

"Can you help me?" William asked.

Salem said, "Sure I can. Your mother and father are waiting for you. Come this way! Follow my voice!"

William got up. "I can't see you," he said.

"You don't need to. Follow my voice. If you can't hear me, look up in the sky. Can you see the Big Dipper?"

"The what?" William asked.

Salem tried to remember what people in the South used to call the Big Dipper. "The drinking gourd made out of stars," he said. "Do you see it?"

"I see it," William said.

"If I have to leave you, William, you run toward the drinking gourd as hard as you can. You just keep your eyes on those stars and keep running. Someone will find you."

"All right," William said. "I'm not afraid now."

They hurried through the dark. With his night vision, Salem saw the woman with the strong voice. She was hurrying toward them along the road. Salem said to William, "Keep going! You'll be safe in a minute." Then Salem slipped off the road.

William passed him. A second later, Salem heard the woman say, "Child, you almost scared your mama to death! Come on, now! We have to run!"

"Yes, Mrs. Tubman," William said.

Salem grinned. Harriet Tubman! That's who the strong-voiced woman was. She had been a slave herself. She escaped to freedom, and in the 1850s, Harriet Tubman made many trips back to the South to help other slaves escape. Some people called her "the Black Moses."

Just then Salem heard another sound. His head whipped around. Not far away,

some men were riding horses along the road. *That's the patrol!* Salem thought. *They're going to catch Mrs. Tubman and William!*

He ran back the way he had come, toward the sound of horses. Salem knew he had to give the runaways time to escape. What could he do?

Before long, he heard the horses and men coming around a bend. Salem ran off the road and climbed a tree. He crawled out onto a limb.

Six men on horses came into sight. One of them said, "We must be close to them. We'll catch them for sure!"

"I think we ought to whip them all," another man said. "We have to teach these slaves a lesson!"

Not if I can help it, thought Salem. *If there's one thing all cats appreciate, it's freedom!* He called out, "There's a bunch of men on horses! Or is it a bunch of fools on mules?"

The men stopped their horses. The leader said, "Did you hear that?"

"I heard something," another one said.

Salem yelled louder: "I'm as free as I can be. You will never catch *me!*"

"It's one of them!" shouted the leader. "Get him, men!"

The horses turned and came trotting. Salem jumped from the tree and ran a little way into the woods. He stopped and called back, "You couldn't find me if you hunted for a week! Maybe you should seek different employment."

"He's over there!" yelped one of the men. Salem heard the horses crashing through the bushes. He ran.

A few seconds later he turned and called out again: "I'm faster and smarter than a *dog.* But even a dog is smarter than you!"

By then the men were getting angry. Salem heard them roaring. Their horses plunged into the brush. This time Salem had to run really fast!

He did not need to stop and yell again. The men were chasing him. He could usually move silently, but in the woods dry leaves lay on the ground. The men could hear the crackle of Salem's footsteps, and they followed the sound. Soon Salem began to gasp for breath. *Well, anyway, Harriet Tubman and her runaways will escape,* he thought. *I've led this patrol miles off the trail!*

Suddenly Salem ran out of the woods. The moon had come up. In its pale light, Salem saw that he stood on the edge of a cliff. A black river rolled by ten feet below. He felt strange. His skin began to tingle.

"Uh-oh! Cats hate to swim!" he said,

looking down at the river. He turned, but it was too late. He could see the horses coming out of the woods. *At the very least, I might be trampled.*

"Bath time!" Salem yelled. He leaped from the cliff!

He held his breath and waited for the splash. It never came. After a few seconds of falling, Salem relaxed. "So that's what the tingly feeling meant. It meant I was about to move on in the book. I'm out of that chapter! That's two down! How many did Sabrina say she had to study? I can't remember! Where will I land next?"

Chapter 4

Salem gazed down. *Night again? I wonder if I'll* ever *land in a nice summer day!*

Below him the orange and yellow lights of a town appeared. They grew larger and larger. Salem saw some buildings he knew. "Hey—that's Washington, D.C. It looks very old-fashioned, though. No electric lights, just oil lamps and candles. And I seem to be falling right onto the roof of the White House!"

He closed his eyes, expecting to crash. Then he landed with a soft thump. Salem opened his eyes again. "Cool! I went through the roof. I landed inside on a nice soft carpet!"

Salem looked around. It was late at night. The rooms in the White House were dark. From somewhere he heard a clock ticking. Salem wandered from room to room until he heard low voices. He followed the sound.

Salem came to a little nook with a desk in it. By the light of an oil lamp, a strongly built man leaned over a stack of papers, making notes in a book. Salem did not recognize him.

Then from the next room came another man's voice. It was high-pitched and slow: "Ward, what do you think of this? 'Eighty-seven years ago, our country began.' "

The man at the desk did not look up. "That's fine, Abe, if you're teaching history. But you're not. You're supposed to be making a speech."

"You're right. Let me think about it."

Salem padded quietly to the doorway and looked into the next room. Sitting at a table was a tall, lean man with unruly dark hair and a dark beard. He had a thin, wrinkled face. He wore a rumpled white shirt, suspenders, and dark trousers. The man had undone his black tie, and it dangled loosely around his neck. Below the table, his big feet were in soft carpet slippers. He bent over a piece of paper and studied it in the light of another oil lamp. Salem recognized the man at once. Salem thought, *Abraham Lincoln! He was president during the Civil War. I must be in the part of the book that tells about the 1860s.*

Mr. Lincoln sighed and crossed out something on the paper. "I don't know why I have to talk, anyway," he said. "Edward Everett is going to give the real speech. He's the famous orator. They asked me just to say a few words. I don't suppose it really matters."

From the alcove behind Salem, the man called Ward replied, "Sir, you are the president. Everything you say matters." He yawned. Salem looked back over his shoulder. Ward blew out the oil lamp and got out of his chair. The man stretched and murmured, "Good night, sir." He walked away.

As soon as he was gone, Salem leaped up onto his desk. He spotted a desk calendar behind a book. Salem nudged the book away and looked at the calendar. It read "November, 1863."

Ah-hah! Salem thought. *I know this.*

We're right in the middle of the Civil War. The North and the South fought a big battle at Gettysburg, Pennsylvania, in July. In November, President Lincoln delivers the Gettysburg Address when part of the battlefield becomes a national cemetery!

"Eighty-seven years," President Lincoln said in the next room. "Ward, I am as stuck as a donkey between two bales of hay. I don't know which way to go. You see, I want to say a little something in this speech. I want to tell all Americans in the North and in the South how solid our Union is, and what a pity and a shame it would be to break it apart. Is that too much?"

Good thing he can't see me, Salem thought. Salem remembered the way Ward had talked. He changed his voice to imitate the man. "No, sir," he said. "It's a good idea."

"The trouble is that eighty-seven years just doesn't *seem* very long," Lincoln continued. "If I say, 'Eighty-seven years ago our country began,' that won't impress anyone. Nobody will think that's solid. There will be people in the crowd who are eighty-seven years old—maybe even older!"

"I see what you mean, Abe," Salem said. "Eighty-seven is old for a person, but it's pretty young for a country." *And I should know! I'm a few hundred years old.*

"Let me think some more."

President Lincoln was quiet for so long that Salem thought he might have gone to sleep. Salem jumped out of his chair. He went to the doorway and looked through.

The president was sitting with his elbows on the table and his fingers locked.

He rested his bearded chin on his hands. His eyes grew wide when he saw Salem. "Tarnation!" he said. "Ward, where do you think this cat came from?"

Of course Ward did not answer. President Lincoln said, "Here, kitty, kitty."

I have to be an ordinary cat, Salem thought. *I can't fool Mr. Lincoln into thinking he's dreaming. That worked with General Washington, but he was tired. Mr. Lincoln looks wide awake!* Salem walked over to the president. He rubbed against Mr. Lincoln's legs. Mr. Lincoln reached down and scratched his neck. "Do you belong to somebody?" Mr. Lincoln asked. "Maybe you can be my boy Tad's pet. He's sick right now. A pet might cheer him up."

Salem purred.

Mr. Lincoln sighed and gave him one last pat. "Well, I have to write a few words, cat. I'm trying to put together a speech. You run along and find a warm corner to sleep in."

Salem trotted back to the nook. He jumped back up into the chair. He imitated Ward's voice again: "Abe, I've been thinking. Your problem is that you want to show the Union is old and solid. Why not use old-fashioned language to do it?"

From the next room, Lincoln said, "I don't follow you. What do you mean, Ward?"

"Well, sir," said Salem, "you know that the word *score* used to be used to say *twenty.*"

"That's right," said Lincoln.

"Well, sir," Salem continued, "four twenties make eighty. Instead of saying, 'eighty-seven years ago,' why not say, 'four score and seven years ago'? That *sounds* older, even if it's the same thing."

"Hmm," said Lincoln. "Four score and seven years ago, our ancestors—"

"Too fancy a word, Abe," Salem said. "I wouldn't use *ancestors.*"

"You're right, Ward," Lincoln told him, looking out the window. "People know I'm just a plain man. If I started using fancy words, it would be like I was trying to say I'm something I'm not. I might as well put on one of my wife Mary's bonnets and tie blue ribbons in my beard. Plain, simple words are best. How's this? Four score and seven years ago, our fathers brought forth on this continent a new nation."

"Perfect, Abe," Salem said. "That says it in a nutshell."

"Now about slavery," Lincoln said. "I want to tell the people that the United States is not a country dedicated to slavery, but to freedom. In America, everyone should be equal. How do I say that?"

"Just say it, Abe," Salem said. "You don't need my help. You're doing pretty well all by yourself."

"By jingo, you're right," President Lincoln replied. "Here we go: Four score and seven years ago, our fathers brought forth on this continent a new nation, conceived in liberty and dedicated to the proposition that all men are created equal."

"Now you've got it," Salem told him. "That's a rouser, Abe!"

President Lincoln chuckled. "Ward, you know nobody's going to remember a little old speech like this."

"You might be surprised, sir," Salem said with a secret smile. He could remember every word of the famous Gettysburg Address. He also knew Sabrina's classmates were studying it over a hundred years later. "But that's not the point, is it? You are there to dedicate a cemetery

for the brave soldiers who fought and died for freedom. Oh, the world may little note nor long remember what you say there, but it can never forget what they did there."

"That's good, Ward," Lincoln said. "That is really good. Do you mind if I use those words?"

"Not at all, sir," Salem said.

For a few minutes Abraham Lincoln wrote. Salem heard his pen scratching across the page. Then the sounds stopped. Salem could hear Lincoln reading softly to himself. The president's voice rose as he came to the end of the short speech: ". . . government of the people, by the people, for the people, shall not perish from the earth."

"First-rate, Mr. President," Salem said. "That'll get the job done, all right." He twitched his ears. He felt a tingle.

"Thank you, Ward. Well, better get to bed. Be sure to pack your bags for the train trip tomorrow. We're going to Gettysburg."

"Yes, sir," said Salem, and he jumped off the chair.

He wasn't surprised this time when he kept falling. He thought, *I always knew that Abraham Lincoln was a great man. I never knew that he liked cats, though. He was a fine leader and he had excellent taste in animals. No wonder he got his picture on the five-dollar bill!*

Around Salem the air began to grow light. He was falling into a daytime scene at last. *It's about time!* he thought.

Chapter 5

"Whee!" Salem plunged down to a green, grassy hilltop. He landed as lightly as a feather. "Oh, this is a lot better," he said, looking at the countryside. "It's a warm, sunny day, the grass is green, and the trees are full of leaves and flowers. Now, where am I? This doesn't look like New Jersey or Maryland or Washington, D.C. Something tells me I'm back down south in this part of the history book."

Salem set out to explore. He trotted down the hill, through some trees, and across a road. He saw brick buildings ahead. Hurrying on, Salem paused in front of a sign. He looked up at it and read, "TUSKEGEE NORMAL AND INDUSTRIAL INSTITUTE."

That helps, Salem thought. *Now I know where I am—in the sunny state of Alabama. Now, when am I? Hmm. The African-American educator Booker T. Washington founded Tuskegee in 1881. But this school has been here a while. The buildings aren't old, but they weren't put up yesterday!*

Salem strolled onto the grounds. Students saw him. Many of them stopped to pet him or scratch his ears. This seemed to be a very progressive school. The people here clearly appreciated cats!

A building with a square tower caught

his eye. Salem walked over to it and saw from a sign that it was "Science Hall." He waited beside the door, and when a student opened it, Salem zipped inside. "Now to find a calendar," he told himself. "Or some other way to learn what part of history this book I'm in is quizzing me on!"

He looked into classrooms full of students. Then he went down a hall and slipped through an open door. Salem sniffed the air. "A laboratory! This is where science experiments are done."

Footsteps came down the hall, and Salem ducked behind a desk. Two people came in, a middle-aged man wearing a suit and a younger man who was dressed like a student. "So you see," the older man was saying, "I believe that chemistry can help everyone in the South. That's what I hope to explore here."

The student said, "How can chemistry help, though? Will you invent new fertilizers?"

With a laugh, the older man said, "Perhaps. But one way chemistry can help is just to tell farmers the best crops to grow. Do you know what soybeans and peanuts have in common?"

"No, sir," the student said.

"They put nitrogen into the soil," the teacher told him. "Other crops take it out. Now, plants need nitrogen. If a farmer learned to rotate his crops, he would grow more. He might plant cotton or corn one year, and then plant peanuts in the same field the next year. The peanuts would replace the nitrogen the other crops took out."

"But peanuts aren't worth much," the student said. "Most people just feed them to horses and cows."

"Then maybe the trick is to find ways to use peanuts," the teacher said. He took out a pocket watch. "You'd better run on," he told the student. "You're going to be late for your next class."

"Thank you, Dr. Carver," the student said as he left.

Salem's whiskers twitched. *Dr. Carver*, was it? That had to be Dr. George Washington Carver. Salem tried to remember what he knew about him. Dr. Carver was a great chemist. He came to the Tuskegee Institute in the year—what was it?—oh, yes, 1896. For many, many years, he would work there and invent hundreds of new products.

Salem watched the professor walk to the window. The man stood with his arms folded, looking out at the world. "New uses for peanuts," the man said softly. "Let me see. I could use the peanut shells to make cloth, or paper, or packing material. And I could use the nuts to make cookies or candy. Hmm. None of those is exciting, though. I need to think up some use for peanuts that everyone would love."

Dr. Carver turned and caught sight of Salem. He raised his eyebrows. "Now, where did you come from?" he asked.

I'd better not talk, Salem thought. *A scientist would think a talking cat is just too weird!* So he just said, "Meow."

"My, you're a handsome fellow," Dr. Carver said, leaning over to pet Salem.

Good eye! Salem thought.

"Did you decide to come to school for an education? Or maybe you're just hungry. Are you looking for lunch?"

Salem realized that he *was* hungry. He had missed breakfast. He meowed again.

Dr. Carver laughed. "Well, come with

me. I'm having lunch in my office today. I think I might find you a little something to eat." He picked Salem up and carried him out into the hall.

Dr. Carver's lunch was waiting for him on his desk. A tray held three covered dishes. Salem's nose twitched. He could smell delicious aromas. Dr. Carver put Salem on the floor. Then he said, "I'm going to wash my hands. You wait until I get back before you start eating!"

Salem explored the office while Dr. Carver was gone. He found a little bowl of raw peanuts on the corner of the desk. *So he wants to get an idea for ways to use peanuts, does he?* Salem thought. *Well, I know the very product he needs. I'll bet that's what the book is quizzing me about. Let me see if I can get Dr. Carver to say the words.* With his paw, he swiped one of the peanuts out of the dish and dropped it on the floor. He landed beside it, just as Dr. Carver came back. "Let me see what we have here," he told Salem. "Now, here is some very fine ham. Would you like some?"

Salem meowed. Dr. Carver rewarded him by putting a tasty piece of ham on a piece of paper. Salem gobbled it right down. "I'm hungry, too," Dr. Carver said. He buttered a roll and started to eat his lunch.

Salem finished his ham. He licked his lips. Then he started to wonder how he would get Dr. Carver to say the magic words. Salem hit the peanut, making it spin around and around. He chased it across the floor.

"What have you got there?" Dr. Carver asked. He leaned over. "A peanut! Well, maybe that's another use for peanuts. They can substitute for catnip mice."

Salem gave him a look. He held the peanut down with his paws and started to lick it.

"Or they could be toothbrushes for cats," said Dr. Carver. "You're a funny cat. It doesn't take much to make you happy, does it? Just a plain old peanut."

Salem stopped licking the peanut. *Yuck! Peanuts might be tasty, but their shells were like cardboard.* And Dr. Carver still did not have the idea.

Salem sat and thought. Dr. Carver ate his lunch slowly, enjoying each bite. Then as Salem saw Dr. Carver putting butter on another roll, he got an idea.

Salem picked up the peanut in his mouth. He jumped up onto a chair. Dr. Carver made a shooing movement with his hand. "Now, cat, you have had your lunch. Let me eat mine, thank you very much."

Salem was not to be shooed away. He jumped from the chair right up onto the desk, next to the food.

"Get down, cat!" Dr. Carver said sharply. "I don't mind sharing my lunch with you, but I don't want to share the table!"

Salem leaned over and dropped the peanut. Then he jumped down and strutted around the floor proudly.

"You look happy with yourself," Dr. Carver said. "But look what you did, you rascal." He reached out and picked up the peanut from where Salem had dropped it. "You put your peanut right in my butter!"

Salem sat down and stared at him.

Dr. Carver stared at the peanut he held. It had smears of golden butter all over it.

"Peanut . . . butter," murmured Dr. Carver. "Peanut . . . butter." He looked

up, his eyes excited. "Peanut butter! Peanuts are very tasty when they're roasted. If I ground them up very fine, I could make a paste from them. The oil in them would hold the paste together. I could spread it on bread just like butter. I wonder how it would taste?" He jumped up. "I can find out! Thank you, cat. You just gave me an idea."

Salem watched Dr. Carver rush down the hall to his lab. With a nod, Salem thought, *Now he's on the right track. Dr. Carver is going to invent hundreds of useful things. I'll bet nothing he invents will be as tasty as peanut butter, though! Dr. Carver, generations of American kids salute you! They're waiting with their bread and jelly—you make the peanut butter, and they'll all enjoy a delicious snack!*

Salem started to get a tingly feeling.

"I'm about to jump to the next chapter," he said. "I'm still hungry, though. If I have time—"

He jumped back onto the desk. Dr. Carver had left a little ham. Salem finished that off. He also ate the last of the butter. Then he jumped off the desk.

As he expected, Salem once again fell right out of the chapter.

Chapter 6

"I must be getting close to the end of the book," Salem told himself. "I've gone all the way from 1776 to 1896. How much more does Sabrina's teacher expect?"

He zoomed down, down, down. Below him he saw a huge city. It stood on an island. To Salem's alarm, he seemed to be falling into the ocean.

"Oh, no! I'm not a sea cat! I'm a land cat! Help!"

Zzzip! Salem landed—and not in the water. He found himself on a hard floor. Hundreds of feet surrounded him. No, thousands! People were walking every which way. Salem ducked between the people, wondering where he was.

Whoops! Almost got stepped on—excuse me! Coming through! Look out, there! Where in the world have I landed this time? Salem finally found a corner where he could crouch and get his breath. He looked around.

He was in a vast brick building, and it was more crowded than any place he could remember. Thousands of people stood in lines or rested in groups. Many of them wore shabby clothes. Many looked tired and anxious.

Then Salem noticed he could see something very familiar through a window. It was an enormous statue of a woman. The

statue wore a crown that sent rays out against the sky. She carried a book in one hand. The other hand was lifted high in the air holding a torch.

New York! Salem thought. *That is the Statue of Liberty. I must be in New York Harbor! Well, if I can make it out of here, I can make it out of anywhere! It's up to me,* not *New York, New York!*

Just where was he? Where in New York Harbor would he find a great big building full of so many people? He had to be on an island—then he remembered.

"This must be Ellis Island! From 1892 until 1954, this was the gateway to the United States. People who had left their homes in other countries had to pass through here on their way to new lives in the United States."

Salem carefully moved from his corner. He wound in and out of the lines of people. "I remember looking at a picture of Ellis Island in Sabrina's history book once. What did the caption say? 'Here thousands of nameless immigrants first set foot on American soil.' Hmpf. Being nameless isn't so cool."

"What's your name?" someone asked.

Salem flinched. He had been talking to himself. Had someone overheard him? He looked behind him and saw that the woman wasn't talking to him. She looked kind and motherly, and she was leaning over a scared-looking little girl about seven or eight years old.

A man wearing a suit came over. He carried a clipboard. "What's the trouble here, Miss Wilson?" he asked.

The woman straightened up. "This little girl has lost her name tag, sir. I was trying to find out who she is."

"No time, no time!" the man said

importantly. "We have lots of people to process. She will just have to wait."

"But her parents will be worried," Miss Wilson said.

"Then get her to tell you who she is," the man replied. He looked down at the little girl. "Can you talk?" he asked. "Can you speak English? Are you German? Italian? Polish? Russian?"

The little girl just stared at him with huge sad eyes.

"Put her in a waiting room," the man said. "She will just have to wait!"

Miss Wilson sighed. "Come with me, dear," she said. She led the girl away, and the man rushed off with his clipboard.

Nameless immigrant, huh? Salem thought. *We'll just see about that. Everyone ought to have a name!*

He hurried to follow the little girl. Miss Wilson took her to a small room. It had a little table, a bed, and one chair. "Just wait here," Miss Wilson said. She hurried out. She did not notice that Salem had darted inside before she closed the door.

The little girl sat in the chair and stared at Salem with big, green eyes. She looked very sad.

Salem jumped up onto the bed. "Well," he said. "Welcome to America."

The little girl blinked at him in surprise.

Salem winked at her. "America takes a little getting used to," he said. "But you'll like it. It's a great place." He sat on the bed and twitched his whiskers. "Your home was probably nice, too. I'll bet you had friends there. Of course, you'll make lots of new friends in America."

The girl tilted her head. In a very soft, squeaky voice, she said, "I didn't know cats could talk."

"Can't cats talk where you come

from?" Salem asked, pretending to be surprised.

The little girl shook her head. "Irish cats don't talk," she told Salem.

"Ah, you're from Ireland," Salem said.

The little girl nodded. "From County Cork," she told him.

"And I'll just bet your parents are out there waiting for you, aren't they?" Salem asked.

Beginning to sniffle, the little girl shook her head. "I'm all alone," she said. "My mum and da are back in Ireland. They'll come over when they have enough money. They sent me to live with my grandparents in a place called Boston, Massachusetts."

"A fine town, Boston," Salem told her. "You'll like it."

The girl began to cry.

Salem walked to her and put a paw on

her arm. "You're scared, aren't you?" he asked in a gentle voice.

The girl nodded. "Y-yes."

"That's all right," Salem told her. "I'm a cat. Cats are the bravest of all animals, you know. But I'll tell you a secret. Even we cats get scared sometimes." *But don't tell Sabrina or I'll never live it down!*

The little girl smiled. It was just a little smile. "What do cats do when they're scared?" she whispered.

"First, we like to know just *where* we are and *when* we are," Salem said. "You know where we are. This is a big American city called New York. Do you know what the date is?"

"Sure I do," the girl said. "It's the second of May, 1900."

"There you are," Salem said. "You're practically over being afraid. There is one thing left, though. To be brave, we cats

have to know just *who* we are. I am Salem, the handsomest cat in America! Who are you?"

The little girl said something very softly.

"I couldn't hear you," Salem said. "Say it louder, please."

"Bridget," the little girl said. "My name is Bridget O'Connor."

"And a fine name it is, too," Salem said. "Don't whisper it. Say it loud. Be proud of it!"

Laughing, Bridget said, "My name is Bridget O'Connor!"

"That's fine!" Salem said. He thought a moment. "You know, you're not just a nameless immigrant. You're a person! You have a name! You know what I would do?"

"What?" Bridget asked him.

"I'd arch my back, walk right out there, find that man with the clipboard, and tell him my name! Why don't you try that?"

"I'm afraid," Bridget said.

"If I go with you, will you do it?"

Bridget thought for a minute. "Will you tell him for me?"

"Me?" Salem said. "Don't be ridiculous. Cats can't talk."

"You're talking to me," Bridget said.

"You're just imagining it," Salem said with a wink. "Or put it this way—cats talk only to people they really, really like. I'll go with you, Bridget, but you have to be the brave one. You have to say your name. Can you do it?"

Bridget bit her lip. She nodded. "I can," she said.

"Then let's go!" Salem jumped off the bed. Bridget opened the door, and they stepped out into the big, crowded room. The man with the clipboard was hurrying past. He stopped when he saw Salem. "A cat!" he said, sounding angry. "Who let a

cat in here? This is against all the rules! Get this cat out of here!"

Salem looked up at Bridget. He winked. He nodded.

The angry man stooped over and reached to grab Salem. Before he could, Bridget tugged his sleeve. He looked at her in surprise. "You!" he said. "The little girl who can't talk? What are you doing out here?"

Bridget opened her mouth. She shouted, "I have a name! I'm Bridget Mary O'Connor, and I have come to live with my grandfather and grandmother in Boston! Their names are Patrick and Susan O'Connor. I'm not nameless! I'm a person!"

The man opened his mouth. He closed his mouth. He looked as if he had forgotten all about Salem. He looked around. "Miss Wilson! Over here, please!"

Miss Wilson came over. "Yes, sir?"

The man made a note on his clipboard. "This is Bridget Mary O'Connor, Miss Wilson, bound for Boston. Take care of her, please! I can't do everything, you know!"

Miss Wilson smiled. She held her arms open. She picked up Bridget.

Bridget looked over Miss Wilson's shoulder at Salem. She gave him a big wink.

Salem followed. Once they knew who Bridget was, it was amazing how fast everything went. Before an hour had gone by, Bridget was on a ferryboat, with Salem in her lap. Miss Wilson had explained to her that someone would meet her when the ferryboat stopped.

As it came up to the dock, Bridget cried out. "Grandpa! Grandmother! I see them!"

Salem slipped off her lap. He watched her run to meet a handsome man and a pretty woman. He nodded. "Nameless, indeed! Goodbye, Bridget! I hope you have a wonderful life in America!"

Then he felt it again—the tingly feeling. It was different, though. This time Salem didn't fall. He flew up, up, up into the air!

"What now?" he wondered.

Chapter 7

"Whoops! I'm out of the book!" Salem flew through the air and landed on Sabrina's bed. "Whew!" he said. "I'm glad that's over! I've been trapped in there for hours." He looked over the edge of the bed. The book lay on the floor. Its words still rippled back and forth like water in a swimming pool.

Salem heard footsteps outside, and the door opened. Sabrina came in, smiling. "Hi, Salem," she said, tossing her books

onto her desk. "Guess what? I aced my test. I think I got a hundred!"

"So did I," Salem told her.

She looked at him. "What do you mean? That's a strange thing to say. You don't even go to school."

Salem sniffed. "That's what you think. Just living with a teenage witch is an education." He made his voice stern and said, "Now, young lady, you've got to remember to pick up after yourself. A good witch never leaves magic lying around where it might get someone into trouble."

Sabrina frowned. "Huh? What do you mean?"

"The book!" Salem said. "You left that history book lying there with the spell still working. It's a good thing I was here to make sure no one accidentally fell into it."

"Oh, I forgot," Sabrina said. "I can take

the spell off, though. Just a second." She pointed. The blue glow surrounded the book. It flipped and flopped and fluttered, and then it lay still. "Okay. It's just a book again," Sabrina said, picking it up. "No harm done."

"Be more careful from now on," Salem said grumpily.

"I will," promised Sabrina.

"So you got an 'A' on the test, did you?" Salem asked.

Sabrina nodded. "I'm sure I did," she said with a big smile. "I knew the answer to every question."

"Good for you," Salem said. "I'm glad my tutoring helped."

"*Your* tutoring?" Sabrina asked in surprise. "Get real, Salem. You didn't help me at all. It was *my* spell that did the trick."

"That's your story," Salem said. He

leaped to the floor and walked out in a dignified way.

"That is one weird cat," Sabrina said, shaking her head. She looked down at her history book. She blinked. She turned a page, and then another and another and another. "Salem!" she yelled. "Get back in here!"

Salem put his head back inside the door. "Yes?"

"What happened to my book?" Sabrina demanded.

"I don't know what you mean," Salem told her, trying to look innocent.

Sabrina sat on the bed. "Come and look at this."

Salem jumped up onto the bed. Sabrina opened the history book to a chapter about the American Revolution. She pointed to a picture. It showed George Washington in a boat as he crossed the

Delaware River to fight the Battle of Trenton. Washington stood in the boat, and just in front of him sat a proud-looking black cat. The cat's head was high. His ears stood up. He stared ahead with an expression of courage.

"What's wrong with it?" Salem asked. "It's a very good picture, if you ask me."

"What's wrong?" Sabrina repeated. "Salem, this is *you* in the picture! I don't think the other history books at school are going to have a cat in them!"

"Maybe they should," Salem said. "An attractive cat or two would improve any book."

Sabrina turned the pages. "What about this one?"

Salem looked down. The picture showed Harriet Tubman leading a band of runaway slaves down a moonlit road. Behind them, running toward a group of

men on horses, was Salem. "Handsome cat," he said. "Maybe a relative."

"It's you, Salem!" Sabrina said. "How about this?"

She turned to a photograph of Abraham Lincoln. Lincoln sat in a chair. At his feet a black cat lay curled up, gazing at the camera. Sabrina turned more pages. A picture of George Washington Carver's lab showed Salem perched on a file cabinet. One of Ellis Island showed Salem being carried by a little girl who held him under his front legs and let his hind legs and tail dangle.

"There's a picture of you in every chapter I studied! What were you up to while I was in school?" Sabrina asked. "And how will I explain this book to my teacher?"

"I was taking my own test while you were at school," Salem said. He jumped off the bed. He looked back over his shoulder. "And if your teacher gets nosy, just say that you have a cat who really went down in history."

"Salem!" Sabrina yelled.

She was too late. Salem had already run downstairs.

Cat Care Tips

#1 Cats should always have fresh food available, since they like to eat frequently throughout the day and night. Cats should eat a good, well-known brand of cat food, since they have very specific nutritional needs. It is fine for them to have snacks of human food if you want to indulge them, but their main diet should always be cat food.

#2 Make sure the cat food you use says that it is completely nutritionally balanced for cats. Try to vary the flavors that your cat receives (unless you have specific instructions from your veterinarian). Cats should not have tuna fish flavor too often.

#3 Never, never let your cat go on a food fast—if he or she does not eat the type of food that you are giving within twenty-four hours you must try another flavor or type of food. Cats will not eat food that they do not like no matter how hungry they get, and they can get very sick if they don't eat for as few as three days. Cats **do not** follow the rule that when they get hungry enough they will eat whatever food you have selected.

—Laura E. Smiley, MS, DVM, Dipl. ACVIM
Gwynedd Veterinary Hospital

About the Authors

Brad and Barbara Strickland are a husband-and-wife writing team. They have written many books together, including some exciting stories for the *Are You Afraid of the Dark, Star Trek: Starfleet Academy,* and *Shelby Woo* series.

Brad teaches English at Gainesville College. He likes to do photography, and he is an amateur actor. Barbara teaches second grade at Myers Elementary School. She likes sewing, reading, and most of all, traveling.

Brad and Barbara have two children. Their names are Jonathan and Amy. They also have many pets, including two dogs, five cats, and a couple of ferrets. With all those animals around, they can understand how Salem thinks! Fortunately, none of their cats is a witch—as far as they know.